Obsession

L.A. Connections 2

Jackie Collins is the author of seventeen provocative and controversial bestsellers. 200 million copies of her books are in print in over forty countries. Jackie Collins lives in Beverly Hills, California, and is currently working on a new novel.

Jackie Collins

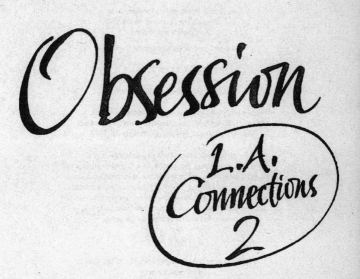

Obsession

L.A. Connections 2

PAN BOOKS

First published 1999 by Pan Books

an imprint of Macmillan Publishers Ltd
25 Eccleston Place, London SW1W 9NF
Basingstoke and Oxford

Associated companies throughout the world

ISBN 0 330 37271 8

5 7 9 8 6 4

A CIP catalogue record for this book is available from
the British Library.

Typeset by SetSystems Ltd, Saffron Walden, Essex
Printed and bound in Great Britain by
Mackays of Chatham plc, Chatham, Kent

The story so far . . .

MADISON CASTELLI, a smart and beautiful twenty-nine-year-old journalist who writes for *Manhattan Style* magazine, sets off for L.A. to interview super-agent Freddie Leon, owner of the powerful IAA agency. On the plane she sits next to Salli T. Turner, a nubile blonde sex symbol, who is busy trying to avoid the attentions of Bo Deacon, a lecherous talk-show host. Madison finds Salli delightfully open and promises to talk to her editor about interviewing her for the magazine.

Salli T.'s husband, Bobby Skorch, a major danger-adventure guy, meets her at the airport, while Madison's old college friend, Natalie De Barge, a popular black TV newsperson, greets Madison and drives her to the house she shares with Cole, her fitness-trainer brother. Both

women commiserate with each other about recent broken
romances.

*

Kristin Carr is an all-American twenty-one-year-old blonde
beauty. She is also a highly successful call-girl, specializing
in rich and famous clients – including Max Steele, Freddie
Leon's partner. Kristin is only doing what she does to pay
the bills to support her sister, Cherie, who lies in a coma
after a deadly car accident two years previously in which her
boyfriend, decadent playboy Howie Powers, smashed his
Porsche into an oncoming truck.

Although Kristin sees Max regularly, she has no idea he
is a friend of Howie.

*

Freddie Leon has problems. One of the stars he represents,
Lucinda Bennett, is refusing to sign her new contract. And
Sam Lowski, her small-time manager, informs Freddie he's
heard that Max Steele is having secret discussions with Billy
Cornelius, chairman of Orpheus Studios. According to Sam,
word is on the street that Billy Cornelius is planning on
dumping his current studio head, Ariel Shore, and giving
the job to Max. Freddie is livid that Max is plotting to leave
IAA without telling him.

*

Natalie's gay brother, Cole, arranged for Madison acciden-
tally to bump into Max Steele at the jogging track. Madison
is delighted as she needs to speak to him for her piece on

Freddie. She has breakfast with him, but he seems determined her interview should focus on him.

*

While shopping at Neiman Marcus, Kristin connects with Jake, a laid-back, extremely attractive award-winning photographer, who has recently relocated to L.A. Charmed by her, and unaware of her profession, Jake invites her out on a date.

They have a great time, but Kristin is smart enough to realize that this is a relationship that can go nowhere.

*

Madison lunches with Salli T. Turner at Salli's glorious Pacific Palisades mansion, with a view to writing an article on the sexy young star. The interview goes well. Madison likes Salli, and her refreshingly honest take on Hollywood and the men in power.

*

Freddie's long-suffering wife, Diana, is throwing one of her much-anticipated dinner parties. The guest list includes Lucinda and her current lover, Dmitri, along with Max Steele, who is bringing gorgeous supermodel, Inga Cruelle, the latest object of his desire.

Freddie drops by Lucinda's house and persuades her to sign her contract. Then, at the last moment, he calls his wife and insists that she invite Ariel Shore, the current studio head of Orpheus, to their dinner party. Diana is not pleased.

*

Jake calls Kristin the day after their date, and invites her to join him at a family dinner. She stalls, nervous about getting involved with him. Then she tells him maybe she will, before leaving her apartment to rendezvous with a mysterious client, Mr X, whom she has seen twice before and instinctively has bad feelings about.

Mr X is an enigma, a man who always dresses in black, including shades and cap. One year previously, unbeknownst to Kristin or her madam, Darlene, a man calling himself Mr X arranged an appointment with Kimberly, a young call-girl. Kimberly was never seen alive again.

Kristin sets off to meet Mr X full of trepidation. This will be her third appointment with him, and she promises herself it will be her last.

*

Madison and Natalie go for dinner at Jimmy and Bunny Sica's house. Jimmy is the news anchorman on Natalie's TV station. He introduces Natalie to his old college buddy, Luther, a burly ex-football player – who soon puts a smile on her face. Madison is not so lucky, but just as she is thinking of leaving, Jake, the photographer, who happens to be Jimmy's brother, walks in, and she experiences an instant attraction. She decides to stick around and see what the evening brings.

*

While somewhere in L.A. . . . a horrific and brutal murder is taking place . . .

PROLOGUE

THE BLONDE fell with a sickening thud, the razor-sharp hunting knife cutting through her carotid artery as if it were slicing butter. Blood pumped from her, like oil gushing from an open well.

The woman attempted to scream, her eyes open wide with the fear and knowledge of what was to come next. But when she opened her mouth, blood gurgled out, spilling down her body and soaking her clothes.

Then her assassin struck again, the lethal knife viciously stabbing her breasts.

Once.

Twice.

Three times.

She sighed. A horrible death rattle of a sigh.

And within seconds she was dead.

L.A.
Connections
2

CHAPTER ONE

MADISON CASTELLI'S green eyes regarded Jake Sica with a certain guarded amusement as he entertained his brother's dinner guests with a hilarious story about a recent photo-safari he'd been on in Africa. Jake had a kind of deadpan delivery that caught her attention and attracted her to him, although she had no intention of getting involved again. Not after her last disastrous relationship – absolutely no way.

Madison was beautiful, with her black hair, olive skin and lithe body, but she played down her good looks, preferring to be known for brains rather than beauty. *I'm twenty-nine, a successful writer for* Manhattan Style *and happily single*, she thought, continuing to check Jake out across the dinner table. *So why am I even thinking about this guy? Especially as I only just met him. Plus he doesn't seem at all interested in me – so what's my problem?*

She glanced over at her best friend, Natalie, who'd brought her to the dinner. Natalie and Jimmy Sica, Jake's brother and the host of this party, worked at the same TV station. Jimmy, with his classic good looks and scintillating smile, was the news anchor, while Natalie took care of the entertainment report. Both were enjoying their night off – especially Natalie, who seemed to be making out okay with Luther, a huge ex-football player and old college buddy of Jimmy's.

"You're a hoot," Natalie said to Jake, shooting Madison a sideways why-don't-you-do-something-about-him? look.

Madison did not respond – she wasn't about to encourage Natalie's not-so-subtle matchmaking, even though she did find Jake attractive.

"I love this!" exclaimed Bunny, Jimmy's pretty wife, clapping her hands together like an excited little girl. "We used to entertain all the time in Detroit. What fun we had!"

"We sure did," agreed Jimmy, flashing his perfect smile.

"How about we play charades later?" Bunny suggested, still full of girlish enthusiasm.

"How about *not*?" Jake responded, with a wry grin.

"I'm with you," Madison agreed. She couldn't stand parlour games – probably because she didn't consider herself very good at them.

"Me too," said Luther, pushing his chair away from the table and stretching. "Man, I do *not* get off on all that goofin' around. Makes me feel like some kind of big old fool."

Bunny pulled a face. "It's *my* party," she said petulantly. "I can do what I want."

"Honey!" Jimmy said, slightly embarrassed. "Whyn't we take a vote?"

"Don't want to," Bunny said, pursing her pink lips, her pretty features contorting into a scowl.

"Sweetheart—" Jimmy started to say.

"Don't nag me all the time!" Bunny shrieked, cutting him off, her baby blue eyes flashing sudden major danger signals.

"Oh, good," Natalie murmured, attempting to lighten things up. "A family fight."

Suddenly Bunny jumped up from the table. "I hate you all!" she screeched, before running from the room.

There was a stunned silence.

Jimmy's smile wavered. "She's only kidding," he said, getting up and hurriedly scooting after her.

"Holy *shit*!" Natalie exclaimed, as soon as Jimmy was out of earshot. "What was *that* all about?"

Both Luther and Jake appeared unaffected by Bunny's outburst.

"Nothing," Jake said, with a wide, unconcerned grin. "That was simply Bunny being Bunny – no big deal."

"Yeah," Luther agreed, reaching for a bottle of red wine and refilling everyone's glass. "Nothin' changes."

"Does she usually scream at her guests like that?" Madison asked, surprised at their calm reaction.

"She only throws a fit to get Jimmy's attention," Jake explained. "It's her way."

"Good for her," Madison said crisply, pushing her chair away from the table. "Only *I* don't have to stay around to watch."

"No, no," Luther said, chuckling. "You don't get it.

9

This shit's bin goin' on since college. They'll be back in a minute all cosy an' down each other's throats. It's their thing."

"Well, it's not mine," Madison said, standing up. "Besides, I've got work to do." She stared pointedly at Natalie, waiting for her to get up, too.

Natalie didn't budge.

"I guess I'd better call a cab," Madison said irritably, swearing to herself that tomorrow she'd hire her own car – no more being trapped.

"Oh," Natalie said innocently, as if it had only just occurred to her, "you're in my car, aren't you?"

"Yes, Natalie, I am," Madison said, stifling the urge to strangle her.

Natalie was not about to give up on Luther. "Maybe *Jake's* going your way," she suggested.

Now all eyes were on Jake. Madison was furious, especially as Jake was not exactly leaping up to offer her a lift. "A cab'll be fine," she said stiffly.

"I'll call one," Jake said. "I *would* drive you, but . . . uh . . . I'm kind of expecting someone."

Oh, great, Madison thought. He's got a late date, and Natalie's begging him to drive me home. How embarrassing is *this*?

"Who?" Luther asked, all interested.

"No one you know," Jake replied, picking up his glass and taking a gulp of wine.

Finally Natalie rallied. "I suppose I should be going too," she said, batting her long eyelashes at Luther, waiting for him to stop her.

He got the message. "No, baby," he crooned, giving her a long, slow-burn look. "It's *way* too early for you to leave."

"Gotta get my beauty sleep," she said, doing the eyelash thing again.

"Honey," Luther said, right on cue, "you're so fine you don't *need* beauty sleep."

Oh, God, Madison thought. Do I really have to listen to this?

And then the phone rang, and all hell broke loose.

CHAPTER TWO

ARIEL SHORE was a statuesque brunette in her late forties, with an abundance of charm and a deceptively bland manner. Beneath the wide, welcoming smile lurked an astute woman, who knew the movie business inside out – a woman who could sweet-talk like nobody else and then – if she felt like it – blow a deal right out of the window without a second thought.

Ariel had started her illustrious career in advertising, moved on to marketing, produced a couple of low-budget films, and then she'd caught the attention of Billy Cornelius, who'd championed her rise to head of his studio. Some said Ariel and Billy were lovers. Freddie Leon, the super-agent, didn't believe it for a minute: Ariel was way too smart to sleep with her boss. Besides, Billy's feisty little wife, Ethel, watched him like a bird-dog – ever since he'd nearly left her for a curvaceous starlet with big silicone-enhanced lips and a talent for latching on to other women's husbands. Ethel had seen to it that the girl was run out of Hollywood, forcing her to seek employment (and other women's husbands) in Europe.

Like Freddie Ariel was career driven, which was why the two of them got along so well. They usually managed to have lunch together a couple of times a month at which they exchanged information – a meeting they both enjoyed because they genuinely liked each other.

Freddie greeted her at the door of his house, hugging her close, whispering in her ear how glad he was she'd made it.

"This was very short notice, Freddie," she scolded. "Only for you."

"I know, Ariel," he replied, poker-faced as usual. "I appreciate it."

"So you should. You owe me, Freddie. And I *always* collect."

"Like I doubted it," he answered, thinking that when he told her that Billy Cornelius was planning on replacing her with his erstwhile partner Max Steele it would be payment enough. "Come on in," he added, putting his arm around her broad, Armani clad shoulders.

Ariel nodded and strode ahead of him. She was an assertive woman, with complete confidence in her ability to charm and conquer.

As Freddie followed her into the living room, he wondered how confident she'd feel when she heard of Billy Cornelius's plans to replace her.

Freddie's wife, Diana, stepped forward, greeting Ariel with a weak smile. Although Diana rarely voiced her opinion about any of her husband's business associates, he knew she couldn't stand Ariel, whom she considered brash and overbearing. He also knew that Diana suspected he might be attracted to the striking studio head, and had once accused him of just such a thing. He'd laughed off her suspicions: Ariel was too important for him to sully their relationship with sex.

"Hi, Ariel," Diana said, with about as much enthusiasm as a dead rattlesnake.

Freddie narrowed his eyes: it infuriated him when Diana exhibited attitude.

"Honey!" Ariel exclaimed, ignoring Diana's coolness. "How *sweet* of you to include me." And before Diana could summon up a reply, Ariel was heading in the direction of hot, sexy young movie star Kevin Page.

"I thought you said she was bringing her husband," Diana hissed.

"She's obviously alone," Freddie replied, too preoccupied to bother with trivia.

"This ruins my table placement," Diana seethed, tight-lipped.

"Get over it," Freddie said, completely unconcerned.

Diana favoured him with a hate-filled look, which he ignored.

Later, at the dinner table, all was back on track. Lucinda Bennett, diva supreme, was holding court, telling lurid tales of her early days in Hollywood and how every man on two legs had been after her. Kevin joined in with hilarious stories about a particularly stoned director he'd recently worked with. And Ariel added anecdotes of her own early experiences.

Freddie noted that Max was uncustomarily quiet. Either he was contemplating what he considered his rosy future, or he hadn't got over the obvious snub from Inga Cruelle, the luscious supermodel who was supposed to be his dinner partner. There had been no telephoned apology; she'd simply failed to show.

Earlier, Freddie had cornered Ariel and informed her about Max's plans to take over her job, as he knew them. She was genuinely shocked. "I don't think Billy would make a move like that without telling me," she'd said. "Everything's going so well at the studio. We've had two enormous hits this year."

"*And* a couple of flops," Freddie had reminded her.

"The hits make up for the flops," Ariel had replied, not quite as pleasantly as usual.

"I'm merely telling you what I know," Freddie had said. "I'm planning on talking to Max tonight, and I want you involved. After all, you and I are on the same side."

Ariel had nodded, but Freddie knew she was angry, as well she should be.

He glanced around the table. Diana's other guests were doing fine. The billionaire businessman and his wife, the New York financier and his L.A. mistress were completely enthralled to be in the company of stars. Good, Freddie thought, now both men would owe him favours – exactly the way he liked things to be.

Brock Martin, the head of one of the TV networks, was

also enjoying himself. He had his eye on Kevin Page's date, the young actress Angela Musconni, she of the pouting lips and seductive eyes. Angie was only nineteen, but her knowing eyes signalled promises of wild sensual experience and Brock felt he was in with a chance. "I don't do television," Angie kept on insisting, as he offered her a mini-series, weekly series or, if she preferred, a major development deal.

"Not even for me?" Brock said finally, perplexed by her lack of interest. He considered himself a stud, having started his career as an actor many years ago, and he simply couldn't understand why she wasn't reacting with more enthusiasm.

"Tell ya what," Angie said, her New York twang reverberating along the dinner table, "if I ever *do* decide t'do TV, it'll *only* be for you. How's that?"

Her pronouncement pacified him, and he gave a satisfied smirk. She rewarded him with a seductive smile, while under the table her child-size hand groped its way up Kevin's thigh, searching for his zipper, so she could pull it down and investigate the possibilities. Angie got off on living dangerously.

Kevin slapped her hand away: he was having a good time listening to Lucinda Bennett and didn't need distractions. Freddie had persuaded him to sign for a movie with Lucinda. He'd almost turned it down, wary that Lucinda was too old. Now he had decided she wasn't too old, after all, and he'd made the right move.

"So, Max," Freddie said, quite loudly, "isn't there something you've been meaning to tell me?"

Ariel sat up very straight. A silence fell across the table.

Max jumped to attention. "What would that be?" he

asked, still wondering where the hell Inga Cruelle was. How dare the Swedish bitch stand him up.

"Come on, Max," Freddie said, playing with him. "You and I have never kept secrets."

"Yes, Max," Ariel said, joining in, her voice sounding ever so slightly strained. "There's a rumour going around."

"A rumour?" Max said warily. Where the fuck was *this* leading?

"That's right," Ariel said, honouring him with one of her most charming smiles. "A rumour that you're after my job."

CHAPTER THREE

DETECTIVE CHUCK TUCCI hitched up the waistband of his moss green pants, which were uncomfortably loose: over the last six weeks he'd lost twelve pounds – thanks to Faye, his wife, who, much against his will, had put him on a rigid diet. He hadn't wanted to lose weight: he was forty-nine, six feet tall and perfectly happy at two hundred and twenty pounds. But Faye had insisted, nagging him about his heart and cholesterol level, and all kinds of ominous ailments. He wouldn't have taken any notice of her, but when she said he felt too heavy lying on top of her when they made love, he'd decided he'd better acquiesce. Hence the diet. Hence the loose pants. Hence his bad mood.

The murdered blonde lay before him in a pool of thick, crimson blood. Another dead body. Another brutal murder.

Only this time things were different. This time the victim spreadeagled on the ground was extremely famous.

Detective Tucci stared down at the once gorgeous woman, her half-naked body vulnerable and exposed, the clothes ripped from her body in a frenzy of violence. Somebody had hacked her to death, almost severing her right breast, viciously stabbing her at least seventeen times.

The white dress she'd been wearing was in blood-splattered shreds around her. No underwear in sight. Blonde pubic hair shaved into the shape of a heart. A small tattoo of a colourful bird just below her pierced navel. Fashionable metallic blue polish on her finger- and toe-nails. She was a beauty.

As he took in the details he let out a deep, weary sigh. This was not his first violent murder; it was his twenty-sixth. However, it was his first famous one.

On his way into the well-appointed living room, with its sweeping views from the huge glass windows, he'd passed a portrait of the victim. Young, blonde, pretty. Like a top-of-the-line Barbie doll, her youthful body captured in a giant nude painting hanging on the wall.

Now she was dead, gone, her sexy image for ever frozen in time.

The police photographer arrived, and started setting up his camera and harsh, glaring lights. He nodded at Detective Tucci and soon began his grisly work, photographing the woman's body from every possible angle, while several cops wandered all over the house, sealing off some areas.

Detective Tucci was particularly concerned with the security outside the house, for he was well aware that once the news hit the airwaves the press and TV crews would descend, swarming around like packs of particularly ravenous vultures. Bad enough when the victim wasn't famous. This time it would be a circus to rival the Nicole Simpson/Ron Goldman/OJ débâcle.

Salli T. Turner. Pneumatic princess of the small screen. Bountiful blonde with the amazing body and sweet, sweet smile. The girl in the black rubber swimsuit.

Adorable girl.

Dead girl.

He continued gazing down at her lifeless, mutilated body and sighed again. Sometimes he thought Faye was right: it was time to retire and get out of the violence business once and for all.

This was one of those times.

L.A.
Connections
2

CHAPTER FOUR

"I CAN'T BELIEVE IT!" Madison gasped, barely able to absorb the shocking news. "It's impossible. I was with her only a few hours ago. There has to be some mistake."

"No mistake," Jimmy said grimly, his handsome face alive with the scent of a sensational story.

"Our boss never makes a mistake," Natalie agreed, agitated because she hated violence and backed away from covering any stories that even touched on it. Now she was stuck, because she and Jimmy had been summoned to their TV station to get a handle on the case.

Madison shook her head, still trying to get her mind around the horrifying news. Salli T. Turner. So alive, vibrant and sweet. It seemed impossible that she was dead, gone, brutally murdered.

"I'm sorry," Natalie said quietly. "I know you liked her."

"I did," Madison said, in a low voice. "How exactly did it happen?"

Jimmy shrugged. "All we know is she was stabbed to death in her house."

"Is it on the news?"

"It will be by the time we get there."

"How did your people find out?"

"Our news director has someone in the police department. We hear everything early." He turned to Natalie. "C'mon, kiddo, we'd better get going."

Reluctantly Natalie picked up her purse, and they all trooped into the front hall.

Bunny emerged from the bedroom and stood with her arms crossed, glaring in sulky silence as everyone prepared to leave.

"You'd better take my car," Natalie said to Madison. "That's if you're okay to drive. I'll go with Jimmy and catch you at home later."

"No," Madison answered quickly. "I should go with you. I'm probably one of the last people to see Salli alive, the detectives will want to talk to me."

"She's right," Jimmy agreed, ignoring his wife's baleful glares.

"Hey," Luther joined in, "what can *I* do?"

"You can call me later," Natalie said ruefully. "I'll need some kind words. Right now I'm totally freaked."

"Me too!" Bunny burst out, lower lip quivering. "This stupid murder has completely spoiled our dinner party."

Madison exchanged glances with Natalie. Jake shook his head. Jimmy threw his wife a furious look, grabbed her arm, and marched her back into the bedroom. Everyone could hear his angry growl – "Do you *always* have to talk like the town idiot? Why can't you keep your mouth shut for once?"

The uncomfortable silence in the hall was broken by the sound of the doorbell.

"I'll get it," Jake said, throwing open the front door. And there stood Kristin Carr, a tentative, slightly nervous smile on her glowing girl-next-door face.

"Uh . . . hi," Jake said, pleased to see the woman he'd only had one date with, but with whom he was definitely enamoured. "Didn't think you'd make it."

Kristin glanced past him, took in the group of people in the hall, immediately noticed two women; an attractive, dark-haired one, and a pretty black woman who looked familiar. *Oh, God*, she thought, swallowing hard, *I hope they're not women I've partied with. I'll die if they are.* She couldn't stand Jake's surprise and disappointment, for he had no idea she was an extremely successful and much in demand call-girl. "I guess I'm late," she said, standing awkwardly in the doorway.

"Not at all," Jake replied, blocking her way into the house, thinking that he wanted to get her out of there so he could have her all to himself. "In fact, you're right on time for me to take you for a drink."

"But I thought—" she began, wondering why he didn't invite her in.

"Everything changed," he interrupted, speaking fast. "I'll explain later."

"Fine," she said, feeling as if she'd walked into an uncomfortable situation, exactly what she *didn't* need after

25

her gruelling session with Mr X – a particularly demanding client who was into mind trips. She sighed, trying to erase from her memory the experience of stripping naked in the back of the limo and pretending to pleasure herself as per the chauffeur's instructions. Of course, the chauffeur was Mr X, no doubt about *that*. He paid exorbitant money, and she had her sister to look after. How else could she pay the enormous nursing home bills?

"C'mon, let's go," Jake said.

"Wait up, bro," Luther interrupted, elbowing his way past Jake. "Don't we get to meet this fine lady?"

"Sure you do," Jake said easily, knowing that a fast exit would've been too simple.

Jimmy emerged from the bedroom. "We're outta here," he said brusquely. Then he, too, noticed Kristin, and stopped short. "He–*llo*," he said, turning on the well-known Sica charm.

Jake moved between them, aware of what a lecherous bastard Jimmy was. "My brother," he said. "Jimmy, say hi to Kristin."

Kristin took a step backwards: civilians always made her edgy – especially this group.

Jimmy was busy flashing his perfect anchorman smile. "And where has my brother been hiding you?'

Kristin recognized the type. She also recognized this man from the TV news, and that made her even more nervous. "Uh . . . away from you, I guess," she mumbled, grabbing Jake's arm, wishing she was someplace else.

Madison observed the scene. It didn't take a genius to realize that Jake was off the market. He definitely had eyes only for this fresh-faced blonde dressed all in white. "Are we leaving or not?" she asked Jimmy impatiently. The journalist in her had kicked in, and she was not interested in anything except finding out what had happened to Salli. She was *certainly* not interested in Jake Sica.

Jimmy took his eyes off Kristin and jumped to attention. "You got it, Madison," he said. "We're on our way."

"Good," she said. And, along with Natalie, they left the house.

L.A.
Connections
2

CHAPTER FIVE

THIS WAS not at all how Max had planned it. He should have known his karma was bad when Inga failed to show. Now he had Ariel on his case with her big phoney smile and faintly Southern accent. Another bitch. Truth was, they were all bitches – the only honest woman he'd ever encountered was his once-a-month hooker, Kristin. At least he knew exactly where he stood with her. Money on the table up front and unbelievable sex.

He decided to play it dumb. Stonewall both Freddie and Ariel. Screw it, he didn't have to answer to anyone.

"What?" he said, quite rudely, so they'd both get the message they were pissing him off.

"I said," repeated Ariel, refusing to back down, "there's a rumour going around that you're campaigning for my job."

Shit! Someone had loose lips. Billy Cornelius had promised him total secrecy until they were ready to make their announcement. Bluff it out, he decided, that was the only way to deal with it.

"I'm flattered that you think I could handle your job," he said calmly. "Truth is, I can barely handle my own." Self-deprecating laugh. Quick glance at Freddie. The ball was now on their side of the court.

Diana, who was totally ignorant of what was happening, did not like the way the conversation was going. She sensed trouble and was not about to let it disrupt her dinner party. "What are you all talking about?" she asked impatiently.

Freddie threw her a look. She caught his displeasure and decided to shut up. Freddie was not pleasant when he was angry: he had a violent, out-of-control temper.

"Beats me," Max said, with a casual shrug.

"You know, Max," Ariel said icily. "I always *knew* Freddie was the heart of IAA. You were merely the gofer with whom people dealt when they couldn't reach *him*." A meaningful pause. "How *sad* always to come second."

The guests at the dinner table fell silent. Even Lucinda was quiet, preferring to listen to the drama taking place rather than continue charming everyone with her fascinating stories of Hollywood past.

"Fuck you, Ariel," Max spat out, regretting the words the moment they left his mouth. Cool was everything, and he'd just blown it.

"That's enough," Freddie interjected angrily. "This is

neither the time nor the place to get into this kind of a discussion."

"*What* discussion?" Max blustered, red in the face. "I'm supposed to sit here while Ariel accuses me of all kinds of shit, and then insults me? Oh, no, Freddie, it ain't gonna happen."

Freddie rose from the table. It was time to put Max firmly in his place. "Come into the library, Max," he said, his face impassive. "We'll talk in private."

"Got nothing to talk about," Max replied, hating the whiny tone he heard in his own voice.

Diana stood also. Damn Freddie, she thought. He'd planned the whole thing. He'd *wanted* to humiliate Max in front of everyone so that the Hollywood rumour mill would gossip about what an asshole Max Steele was, and how Freddie Leon had caught him with his pants down.

Well, she was not going to stand for it. Max deserved better. He'd always been a good friend to her, and in spite of his appalling taste in women, she liked him and she suspected he liked her. In fact, if she weren't married it was quite possible that she and Max might have got together.

The very thought brought a blush to her cheeks. Abruptly she left the dining room and marched into the kitchen, where the help and the caterers were all gathered around the small portable TV.

"What *is* going on?" she demanded, not pleased that they were slacking off when they should have been hard at work.

Ronnie, her regular barman, black and capable, a middle-aged veteran of the more upscale Hollywood parties, stood to attention. "Breaking news, Mrs L," he said excitedly. "Big murder in the Palisades."

Diana frowned. "I couldn't care less *who*'s been murdered," she said tartly. "We have a dinner party in progress. Kindly get back to work immediately. And that's an order."

L.A. Connections 2

CHAPTER SIX

DETECTIVE TUCCI was still contemplating the body of the murdered actress when Officer Andy Flanagann sidled up alongside him. Officer Flanagann had been the first person on the scene – summoned by a neighbour complaining about barking dogs and loud music. By the time Detective Tucci had arrived there, the dogs were locked in the kitchen and the music turned off. Nothing else had been touched.

Tucci thought Andy Flanagann was too young for the job – still he had a fresh-faced enthusiasm, and at least he seemed competent.

"You'd better come with me, Detective," Officer Flanagann muttered, avoiding looking at Salli T. Turner's mutilated body.

"What's up now?" Detective Tucci asked, his stomach rumbling.

"Another victim," Officer Flanagann said flatly. "Male. Shot in the face. Discovered the body outside the guest house."

"Jeez!" Detective Tucci exploded, thinking, *There goes dinner.* A double homicide was always twice the work and twice the aggravation – especially when both murders were committed by different means. A stabbing and a shooting. Perfect.

"Sorry," Officer Flanagann mumbled, like it was his fault.

Detective Tucci hitched up his pants again and, armed with a heavy-duty flashlight, followed the young officer across the floodlit lush green lawn surrounding an azure blue swimming-pool. Salli T. Turner must have worked hard to afford such a palatial spread, he thought. Their path was dotted with giant palm trees, potted bougainvillea, fragrant peach and lemon trees. Some people really knew how to live. Pity they had to die before their time. Especially like this.

Tonight Faye was making turkey meatloaf with her secret salsa sauce – a special treat. Detective Tucci forgot about his diet for a moment and imagined her taking the pan out of the oven, leaving it to cool while she called him into the kitchen to eat. Ah, yes, he'd leave his precious Lakers, and race to her side. Faye was a good cook, and at forty-two still a most attractive woman. Fiery, too. But, then, she was half Hispanic, with jet-black hair and a pocket Venus body. They'd been married five years; his first wife had died of cancer. He loved Faye very much.

"It looks like one bullet," Officer Flanagann offered.

"Seems like the victim might have been on his way to the main house to investigate the noise."

Detective Tucci nodded. Amateur detectives irritated him. It was his case, he'd solve it, he didn't need any help.

The male victim was sprawled on his side, half on the walkway and half on the grass leading from the guest-house. He had no face, just an angry mud-patch of blood and bones.

It was not the first time Detective Tucci had seen someone who'd been shot in the face. It was never a pretty sight. His stomach churned – this time not from hunger – and he wished he was at home.

Carefully aiming his flashlight, he studied the body. Male. Slight and skinny. Clad in psychedelic shorts and a midriff-baring white tank. Pierced navel. Glossy black shoulder-length hair. Oriental hair.

Detective Tucci leaned closer, his torch skimming up and down the lifeless body.

"No weapon," Officer Flanagann said helpfully. "I checked all around."

"Did you go in the guest-house?"

"The door was open. I inspected the premises. It does not appear to be a home invasion."

Detective Tucci stared at the body. "Houseman," he said, thinking aloud. "Get the photographer down here. And make sure nothing's touched. Got it?"

"Yes, Detective," Officer Flanagann said, jumping to attention. "Don't you worry. I'll take care of everything."

CHAPTER SEVEN

KRISTIN SAT next to Jake in a booth at the bar in the Beverly Wilshire Hotel. He'd ordered a beer, and she was sipping Evian. Both of them were treading carefully.

"I'm really glad you came by," Jake said, trying hard not to stare, for she was truly gorgeous in a refreshingly wholesome way. "I was beginning to kind of wonder if you'd show."

"Did you think I would?" she asked, feeling for once like a real girl on a real date and liking it.

He shrugged. "Wasn't sure," he answered honestly.

She smoothed down the skirt of her white dress with the palms of her hands. "Can I ask you something?" she ventured, studying the way his eyes crinkled when he smiled.

"You can ask me anything you like."

She hesitated a moment. "Uh," she began, not even

embarrassed because she was determined to know, "I noticed two attractive women in the hall. Was one of them with you?" *Why am I asking him this?* she thought. *I hardly know him. And yet . . .*

"Oh, sure," he said, laughing. "Like I'd invite you over to join me and my family, and there I'd be with a date." His brown eyes were full of amusement. "C'mon, Kristin, what kind of a guy d'you think I am?"

"A nice guy," she answered softly.

He took a swig of beer. "Now you're making me sound boring."

"No, I'm not."

"Yes, you are."

They grinned at each other. He was delighted she'd wanted to know whether he was with Natalie or Madison: it showed that maybe she cared.

"Your brother's on television, isn't he?" Kristin asked, carefully picking a slice of lime out of her drink.

"Jimmy's a news anchor."

"I recognized him."

"He'd like that. His ego's bigger than his brain."

"Do you two hate each other?" she asked curiously.

"Naw. He can be a real jerk, but he's still my brother."

"And so the two of you are going to your father's wedding?"

"Wouldn't miss it. My dad's the character of all time." A beat, then, "Hey – why don't you come?"

She shook her head, natural blonde hair swirling around her pretty face. "I don't think so."

"Why not?" he asked, hoping he might persuade her to say yes. "We could have fun."

"I'm not used to having fun," she said quietly.

He looked at her quizzically. "What does *that* mean?"

"I work all the time," she said, tapping her clear polished nails on the table. "My sister was in a bad car accident. She's been in a coma for over two years."

Impulsively he took her hand. "You poor kid."

"No," Kristin said fiercely. "*She*'s the poor kid. *I*'m the one who's still able to walk around."

"Does that mean you have to support her?"

"I don't *have* to do anything," she said, her voice tightening as she withdrew her hand from his.

"What about your husband? Doesn't he help out?"

A moment of silence. "I . . . uh . . . wasn't quite truthful with you, Jake," she lied, remembering the fictitious rich husband she'd made up to protect herself. "I left my husband six months ago. He doesn't pay me a dime."

"Then you're single?"

"Separated."

He fixed her with a long, penetrating gaze. "Glad to hear it."

"Why?"

"Now isn't that a silly question?" he said, teasingly.

She lowered her eyes, his gaze was too intense for comfort.

"So . . . tell me, Kristin," he continued, "are you currently involved with anyone?"

She was silent again. Was sleeping with a variety of men

rich enough to pay for her exclusive services the same as being "involved"?

No. That was business.

And business and pleasure do not mix.

A harsh reminder that she shouldn't be sitting here with a man whom, undeniably, she found attractive.

"Hey," Jake said, pushing gently, "do I get an answer?"

"I . . . I don't have time to be involved," she said. "Have to keep working to pay the bills."

"That's *not* a healthy attitude."

She shrugged, studying his lips, wondering what it would be like to kiss them. "I know," she said. "But what can I do?"

"Spend more time with me for a start," he said, playfully. "I'm new in town. I need a tour guide, someone to show me what *not* to do."

"I *am* spending time with you."

He took her hand again and she experienced long-lost shivers of desire. "I've never met anyone quite like you, Kristin," he said, his brown eyes sincere and probing. "Are you feeling the same way I am?"

She nodded, unable to stop herself, even though she knew she was venturing into dangerous territory.

"Then why don't we do something about it?" he suggested.

"Like what?" she murmured, knowing full well what he meant.

"My hotel or your place?" he said, deciding to go for it.

Her place was her sanctuary; she never took clients there.

Only Jake *wasn't* a client. He was a man she desperately

wanted, and maybe if she slept with him she would get over her overwhelming desire for him, and then normal life could resume.

"My place," she whispered, still flushed with excitement.

He squeezed her hand. "I'll get the check."

CHAPTER THREE

L.A.
Connections
2

CHAPTER EIGHT

BY THE time Jimmy and Natalie reached their TV station, news of the Salli T. Turner murder was spreading across L.A. like an out-of-control brush fire, which really pissed Jimmy off because he'd expected to be first to announce the killing on air.

Madison followed them into the news room, still dazed by the shock. She kept on thinking of Salli as she was when they had had lunch earlier in the day – so vibrant and alive. Now she was dead, and it didn't seem possible.

Garth, the news director, a tall man with angular features and sparse yellow hair plastered to his scalp, was not pleased either. "What the hell took you so long?" he screamed at Jimmy, ignoring both Natalie and Madison.

"I live in the goddamn Valley for chrissakes," Jimmy

retorted, bad-temperedly. "Pay me more money and I'll move closer."

"Never mind," Garth growled. "You're going on a special news break. Get moving."

"Thanks," Jimmy said sarcastically, taking off for the makeup room.

"As for you, sweetie," Garth said, turning to Natalie, "prepare me a eulogy for the eleven o'clock news. Something that'll break everyone's heart *and* keep 'em watching." He licked his thin lips. "We'll use plenty of footage of Salli bouncing along the beach in her sexy black rubber suit. Nothing like T and A and a good murder to guarantee mega-ratings."

"I was thinking," Natalie blurted. "Maybe Madison should do it, she was with Salli today."

Madison threw Natalie an amazed look. "*I'm* not going on TV," she objected. "What's gotten into you?"

Garth took notice of Madison for the first time. "Who're you?" he asked rudely.

"Someone with better manners than you," she shot back, irritated by his brusque attitude.

"Madison's my journalist friend from New York," Natalie explained quickly. "She flew out on the same plane as Salli. And today she was at Salli's house having lunch."

Garth's long, thin nose smelt an exclusive. "You *were*?" he asked, practically salivating.

"That's right," Madison replied curtly. "And I can assure you I have absolutely *no* intention of talking about it on TV."

"Why not?" Garth demanded.

Madison frowned. What was wrong with Natalie? Why was she trying to use her? And who was this total *idiot*? "Don't you people care that a beautiful young woman has been *murdered*?" she said furiously. "What is this to you? Nothing more than a ratings race?"

"Now, now," Garth said gently. "Understandable you're upset. But the public has a right to know. As a journalist, you should understand that."

"Sorry," Madison said shortly. "I don't think they have a *right* to anything."

Garth scratched his head. There was nothing worse than a stubborn woman – especially a stubborn female journalist. "How much?" he asked wearily, as if money could solve any problem.

"How much what?" she said, still frowning.

"Money. For you to get on air."

She gave him an icy glare. "You just don't get it, do you?"

"No, honey," he answered patronizingly. "It's *you* who don't get it. News is news, and if you *were* with her today, we're sitting on dynamite. So tell me what it's gonna take to get you in front of the camera?"

Madison couldn't believe what a moron this guy was. "Nothing *you* have to offer," she said, dismissively.

"Drop it, Garth," Natalie said, sensing that Madison was about to lose it. "It was a dumb idea. Sorry, Maddy."

"No, honey," Garth sneered. "For once you got it right."

"Hey," Madison said, directing her words to Natalie, "I'm out of here. You work for this asshole, *I* don't."

"Who're *you* calling names?" Garth said, a plum red flush spreading up from his neck.

"Forget it," Madison said. "Let's just say it wasn't a pleasure."

"Maddy—" Natalie began. But it was too late: Madison was on her way out.

Angrily she made her way to the front desk and requested the young man at reception to order her a cab. Then she used her cellphone to reach her editor, Victor Simons, in New York, where it was now one thirty in the morning.

"Listen to me, Victor," she said, her words tumbling over each other as she was overcome with a sudden rush of adrenaline.

"What?" Victor mumbled, half asleep and disoriented. "It better be important."

"It is," Madison said. Reluctantly she acknowledged she *did* have a hot story, and she'd better pursue it. "Salli T. Turner was murdered tonight. Stabbed to death."

"You sure?"

"*Very* sure."

"Weren't you having lunch with her today?" Victor asked, sounding a lot more alert.

"Yes. I was at her house earlier."

"Then it must've—"

"—happened after I left," Madison said, finishing the sentence for him.

"You should—"

"Don't worry, Victor, I'm on to it. In fact, I'm heading for the murder location right now. Expect to hear from me later."

L.A.
Connections
2

CHAPTER NINE

MAX STEELE was not about to be lectured to by the likes of Freddie Leon – "the Snake", as everyone referred to him behind his back. Screw Freddie. Screw 'em all. Max was on an I-hate-everyone roll.

The plain truth was that Ariel was right: people always *had* regarded Freddie as the major partner in IAA; Max Steele always came second. Oh, he knew what they said – "If you can't get to Freddie, settle for good old Max."

Dammit! He'd had enough; he was glad he was splitting. When he was ensconced as studio head he'd be a man to be reckoned with, not some little piss-ant agent. Then everyone would kiss his ass big-time.

Before he'd left, Freddie had made an attempt to edge him into the library. Instead he'd stormed out – he had nothing to say until he'd figured out exactly how he was going to say it.

Now he was in his red Maserati cruising along Sunset, listening to All Saints on his CD player, wondering what the hell he was going to do to calm down.

He shouldn't have pissed Ariel off, he knew that for sure. She was a cunt – but she was a cunt with connections.

No bad karma. That was his new motto.

I need a snort, he thought, *a touch of the magic white powder to calm me down and make me feel smooth as velvet.*

Howie would have what he needed. But hadn't Howie mentioned he was going to Vegas with his old man?

Yeah. Maybe. One never knew with Howie – he was a number-one degenerate fuck-up, typical son of a rich man. Money no problem, there was always more where that came from. Never kept a job for longer than two weeks. Never met a beautiful woman he didn't want to sleep with. Never encountered a drug he wasn't willing to try. Max reckoned Howie had brain damage from all his excesses.

Still . . . you could relax with a guy like Howie, have some laughs. And sometimes Max needed laughs when business got too intense.

He pulled his Maserati up outside Riptide on Sunset and left it with an eager valet. Max was known around town as an excellent tipper.

Riptide was the latest place to hang – a restaurant club with good food, crowded bar, and many beautiful, available women. Not that beautiful, available women were hard to come by in Hollywood. Truth was, they were everywhere, would-be models and actresses who flocked into town hoping to become the next Pamela Anderson or Claudia Schiffer, and ended up posing for *Playboy* or getting walk-ons in some horny producer's movie. Then there were the women who'd made it, the television stars with their own series, and the supermodels with their lucrative cosmetic contracts. And, above all of them, were the mega-stars such as Sharon Stone, Michelle Pfeiffer and Julia Roberts, talented females who'd gotten to the top in spite of the odds.

Max liked to sample all levels. Howie usually settled for the would-bes, claiming they were more grateful.

Bianca, Riptide's shapely Brazilian maître d', greeted him warmly – as well she should: he'd gotten her the job after a night of interesting sex on a friend's yacht in the marina. Banking favours was Max's speciality.

"Hi, Max – joining Howie's table?" Bianca asked, gold hoop earrings jangling from exceptionally small earlobes.

"Thought he was in Vegas," Max replied, giving her a friendly pat on her black-satin-clad ass.

"He's here," Bianca said, leading him through the crowded restaurant. "You know," she said, over her shoulder, "I can't believe the news about Salli T. Turner. She was in here all the time with that shit-heel husband of hers. I wouldn't be surprised if *he* was the one who did it."

"Did what?" Max asked blankly, waving at various friends and acquaintances as he trailed Bianca through the room.

She stopped short. "Haven't you heard?"

"What?"

"Salli was stabbed to death," Bianca said, in a horrified

whisper. "They're saying whoever did it cut off one of her breasts."

Max shuddered. "Jesus!"

"It's so horrible! Did you know her?"

Max nodded, remembering the time Salli T. had come to the office with the intention of seeing Freddie. Naturally Freddie was completely uninterested, so Max had ended up feeling sorry for her, and taken her for a drink in the bar at the Peninsula where he'd given her career advice. In return she'd offered him a blow job. He'd turned her down. Not his type. Too obvious with the fake boobs and cascades of platinum hair. But sweet with it, almost naïve in a way.

"When did this happen?" he asked.

"Earlier tonight," Bianca answered. "I'm getting myself a gun. If it can happen to her it can happen to anyone."

"Now, don't go getting paranoid," Max said, not mentioning that he'd had a hidden compartment specially built into his Maserati to house a fully loaded Glock.

"Why not?" Bianca demanded, dark Brazilian eyes flashing. "It's the truth."

"Was it a break-in?"

"Nobody seems to know. It's all over the TV."

And then they were at the booth. And there sat Howie in a three-thousand-dollar Brioni suit, four-hundred-dollar Lorenzini shirt, and a hundred-and-fifty-dollar Armani tie. There was nothing cheap about Howie – especially when he was spending his old man's money.

On the table in front of him was a half-empty bottle of Cristal in a silver ice-bucket, with two glasses and a large glass dish filled to the brim with the best Beluga caviar.

Lounging next to Howie on the comfortable leather banquette was Inga Cruelle, Max's erstwhile date, a blank expression on her perfect, supermodel face.

"Jesus!" Max exploded.

This was not turning out to be his perfect day.

L.A.
Connections
2

CHAPTER TEN

ANGELA MUSCONNI was bored. She'd had enough of watching the goings-on at the grown-up table. She was nineteen years old, for chrissakes, too young to sit around with a bunch of boring old farts.

Kevin Page had talked her into coming with him. "C'mon, babe," he'd said persuasively, still impressed with his own sudden fame. "It's a movers-and-shakers deal – we gotta go."

"What do I care?" she'd answered, with a couldn't-care-less shrug. She'd met enough so-called movers and shakers on her way up. They were no big surprise, star fucks, every one.

When she'd first come to Hollywood, nobody had wanted to know her. Oh, yeah, a blow-job was acceptable to certain producers, who'd promised her everything and then forgotten her name. Apart from that, she was treated like a nothing – a dumb little street-kid.

Now they all wanted to suck up to her, including Brock Martin, who really thought he was hot shit on a plate. Of course, Brock didn't remember two years ago when he'd tried to pick her up at Farmer's Market on a Saturday morning, and offered her money for a hand-job. Pervert! Out trolling for teenagers when he had a wife and two kids at home.

She'd been broke at the time and quite tempted; now she could reject him and enjoy watching him beg. But it was only amusing for five minutes. After that, it was a yawn.

She didn't get it. What fun was there in sitting around a fancy dinner table with waiters serving all kinds of gourmet crap, when she and Kevin could be making out, eating pizza or cruising the clubs?

And what was with Kev brown-nosing Lucinda Bennett's saggy ass? She was old enough to be his *grandmother*, for chrissakes.

Angie sighed. Sometimes Kev was so out of it. Even though he was five years older than her, he was not nearly as street smart. If she was planning on staying with him, she'd have to teach him how to operate.

Restlessly she got up from the table. "Goin' to the john," she mumbled. Like anyone cared. Kev certainly couldn't give a rat's ass.

She wandered through the ornate living room, taking in the silver frames filled with signed photos of presidents and movie stars. Then she checked out the expensive art hanging on the walls, tastefully lit. There was a Picasso here, a Monet there. *Bo—ring*.

The only place any sounds were coming from was the kitchen, so she gravitated in that direction. Peeking around the door, she was amazed at the size of the industrial-looking room. Holy shit! The fucking kitchen was bigger than her entire New York apartment!

A bunch of people were busy, busy, busy. Ah, the staff – her kind of people. She'd grown up in New York, where her mom worked as a maid and her dad drove a union truck. Recently she'd moved them from Brooklyn to a house she'd bought them in Paramus. They'd hated it. Too bad.

"Hi, guys," she said, wandering into the enormous space filled with industrial ovens, several dishwashing machines, thick wood-block cutting boards and two giant centre islands. "Can I bum a cigarette?"

Ronnie, the barman, who was stationed in front of the TV, dragged himself away. "Sure, Miss Musconni," he said, groping in his pants pocket for a pack of low-tar Camels. "Only don't smoke it around Mrs Leon, she don't allow smoking in the house."

"Really?" Angie said, with a wicked grin, plucking a cigarette from his crumpled pack. "I'd like to see her try to stop *me*!" She got off on the clout that came with movie-stardom – it gave her a constant high. "Hey," she said, edging nearer the TV. "What's going on?"

"Big murder in Pacific Palisades," Ronnie announced. "Up the street from Steven Spielberg's place. We're watching live coverage from outside the house."

"No shit," Angie said, moving closer to the small screen. "Who got wasted?"

"Salli T. Turner," Ronnie answered, twisting his head to make sure Diana Leon wasn't creeping up on him. Mrs Leon was the most demanding of Hollywood wives: she had a nasty habit of appearing unexpectedly.

Angie's hand flew to cover her mouth. "God, no!" she gasped. "Not Salli!"

"Did you know her?"

"Yes," Angie whispered, her face ashen.

"That's too bad," Ronnie said.

"Who . . . did . . . it?"

"They don't know, Miss Musconni."

"I do," Angie said fiercely. "He always threatened he was going to kill her. Now the bastard has."

"Who?" Ronnie asked, hoping for some inside scoop he could sell to one of the tabloids.

But Angie was already on her way back into the dining room.

*

Diana threw Angela a furious look. Wasn't it bad enough that Freddie had tried to ruin her dinner party by fighting with Max? Now this so-called actress had burst back into the room, telling everyone about the murder.

Diana knew exactly what would happen next: they'd all be dying to go home and huddle in front of their televisions. Damn! Why couldn't Salli T. Turner have gotten herself murdered on another night?

Angie announced the news, then immediately dragged Kevin off, barely saying goodbye.

Good riddance, Diana thought sourly.

Soon all the remaining guests were talking about the OJ case, reliving the most notorious murder trial of the century. Everyone who lived in L.A. had an opinion. But the discussion didn't last long, because after Angela and Kevin's abrupt exit – just as Diana had expected – they all wanted out. Brock Martin was first on his feet, anxious to run over to his TV station. Lucinda was next, television junkie that she was. And Ariel couldn't wait to split.

Freddie was not fazed by everyone making a fast exit, but Diana was seething, although she put on a good act of saying goodbye graciously.

As soon as the last person left, she turned on Freddie. "I don't ask much of you," she said, tight-lipped. "But one thing I *do* expect is that when we're entertaining you behave like a gentleman. My dinner parties are important to me, and you ruined tonight."

"What *are* you talking about?" Freddie snapped, in no frame of mind to suffer one of Diana's moods.

"How dare you air your problems with Max in front of my guests?" Diana said, her voice rising.

His eyebrows rose. "*Your* guests, Diana?"

She backed down. "Our guests," she conceded.

"I hope you're not telling me how to run my business," Freddie said, grim-faced.

"No . . . but Max is your *partner*, your *friend*—"

"Bullshit," Freddie said harshly. "I made him – and let

no one forget it. He thinks he's capable of running a studio. Ha! Any moron could run a studio better than him."

"It'll be in Army's column tomorrow," Diana fretted. "It doesn't make *you* look good."

"Diana," Freddie said coldly, "stay out of my business."

"Fine," she replied, turning her back on him and hurrying upstairs, wondering if any of the staff had overheard their argument. God! That was all she needed. Ronnie, the barman, running around the Bel Air and Beverly Hills circuit telling everyone that the Leons had had a big fight. Freddie was as high profile as any movie star. Mr Super-agent. Mr Power. He was as big as Mike Ovitz had once been, before the débâcle at Disney.

Once upstairs, Diana sat at her dressing-table and wondered what Max was doing now. She understood why he had to leave the agency: it was because Freddie had always kept him in the background – kind of like the court jester. But she knew the truth. Underneath Max's brash exterior lurked a caring, sensitive man. And one of these days she planned on finding out exactly how caring and sensitive he was.

The intercom buzzed. "I'm going for a drive," Freddie said, his tone cold and flat. "Don't wait up."

Not to worry, Diana thought. *I have better things to do with my time.*

L.A.
Connections
2

CHAPTER ELEVEN

JAKE FOLLOWED Kristin into her apartment, looked around, and let out a long, low whistle. "Some place," he said, admiring the expensive décor.

"Uh . . . thank you," she answered nervously. He was right, her apartment *was* nice. And so it should be: working with a decorator, she'd overspent, but the result was soothing and tasteful, exactly what she'd been looking for. She considered her apartment her haven, the one place she could be alone. Now she was bringing Jake – a virtual stranger – into her private domain.

Am I insane? she thought. *Why am I doing this?*

Because you like him.

No, I don't like him. I'm lonely. I need the arms around me of a man who isn't paying me. Is that a crime?

Yes, because you're setting yourself up to get hurt.

"Would you like a drink?" she asked, still feeling ridiculously skittish.

"Wouldn't mind a beer." He laughed. "Bet that's something you don't have."

"It's not my drink of choice, but I can offer you vodka or wine."

"Not a heavy drinker, huh?"

"I never drink by myself."

"So you're a good girl," he said teasingly.

"Now you're making *me* sound boring," she countered.

"Wouldn't want *that*," he said, coming up behind her and putting his arms lightly around her waist.

She turned in his embrace and began to say something, but he stopped her with his lips, and they were as good as she'd known they'd be.

He kissed her for several long, slow-motion minutes. She couldn't remember the last time she'd been kissed, because paid-for sex did not usually involve that kind of intimacy. The sensation was unbelievably heady yet fraught with danger.

Finally she forced herself to push him away. "I need a drink," she whispered.

"So do I," he agreed. "We're both nervous."

"You're nervous, Jake?" she asked, surprised. "Of what?"

"*You* make me nervous. In fact," he added with a rueful grin, "you made me nervous the first time I spotted you in Neiman's."

"I did?"

"You certainly did. I mean, there I was, minding my

own business, searching for a tie. And there *you* were, sitting at the martini bar, looking to break my heart."

"I was not," she objected. "If I might remind you, it was *you* who picked *me* up."

"No. It was *you* who came and sat beside me."

"Liar! Liar!" she said, enjoying the game. "I was already there – *you* sat next to *me*."

"I did?"

"You did."

"Then I must be smarter than I thought."

She laughed softly. "You're so romantic."

"Was your husband romantic?"

"Please don't talk about him," she said, moving quickly over to a side table where she kept glasses, red and white wine and a bottle of vodka. It was not like she ever entertained – the set-up was purely decorative.

Once more, Jake came up behind her. "I'll play barman," he said, taking the vodka out of her hands.

"If you insist," she said, shivering slightly.

He poured them both a healthy shot. "Where's the ice?"

"In the kitchen."

She watched him as he left the room. He was very watchable, tall and lean with a long-legged stride that she found irresistibly sexy. She could hear the jangling of ice cubes as he removed them from the freezer. When he returned he handed her a glass. "Okay, this is the deal," he said. "I'm making a toast."

"To what?"

"To you – because you're beautiful, inside and out."

Oh no, Jake, don't say such things. The truth is that I'm ugly and I never want you to find out.

"I know this is all happening fast," he continued, "but I feel I've got to tell you."

"Tell me what?" she asked, holding her breath.

He took a long beat, then, "This'll sound like another line – only it's the truth. I . . . uh . . . I guess I've never felt this way before."

Oh, God! Please don't get carried away, Jake. Take this for what it is, one night of love. One long, leisurely, unpaid-for night of love.

"How about you?" he demanded, staring at her.

She stalled, pretending she didn't understand. "How about me what?"

"Jeez!" he said, perplexed. "I'm declaring all kinds of true feelings and you're stonewalling me. What's going on, Kris?"

Nobody called her Kris. It felt familiar and endearing. She shrugged. "I . . . I don't know," she murmured. "Something . . ."

"Yeah . . . something," he agreed. And then he was kissing her again, his body pressing hard against hers, his lips insistent and intoxicating.

She felt herself dissolve inside. This was too good to pass up. One night. Didn't she deserve one night of happiness?

Jake's hands slid down her shoulders to her breasts and began fingering her nipples through the flimsy folds of her white dress, causing her to catch her breath. She'd faked sexual excitement for so long that the real thing was almost a surprise. She shivered with anticipation: it was as if she'd never been touched there before.

Slowly he started easing her dress off her shoulders. She leaned back, making it simple for him.

He released her breasts from the thin material and bent to kiss them, rolling his tongue around her nipples in a way that immediately started to drive her crazy. She sighed loudly, knowing for sure that she never wanted him to stop.

"You . . . are . . . so . . . beautiful," he murmured, his tongue continuing to arouse her. "So . . . fucking . . . beautiful."

I'm a professional, Jake, I have to keep in good shape.

"Thank you," she whispered, wondering if it would seem too bold if she went for his belt and pushed down his pants.

"I haven't been with a woman in over a year," he admitted. "Unless sex means something, it's not for me."

Words to stop anyone in their tracks. "I . . . uh . . . can understand that," she managed.

"The reason I'm telling you is so that you know you can trust me."

Trust him? What did he mean? And then she got it. He was telling her he didn't have Aids or any other catchable diseases.

Oh, God, now he was waiting for her to give him *her* sexual history.

Well, Jake, it's like this. I'm a whore. But you can feel perfectly safe because if they touch me I always insist they use a condom. And I visit my gynaecologist twice a month. And . . . oh, shit, why am I fooling myself? This silly charade of falling in love has nowhere to go.

And yet . . .

"I haven't slept with anyone since my husband," she murmured.

"Well, then," he said, obviously pleased with her reply, "you and I are about to make this a night to remember."

CHAPTER TWELVE

THE CAB TOOK MADISON to a late night car-rental office, and now she sat behind the wheel of a green Ford Galaxy, driving towards Salli's house in Pacific Palisades. No more depending on other people to get around this town.

Her thoughts were full of Salli, as she tried to dredge up every detail of their lunch together. She remembered walking into Salli's luxurious house, her sense of how unlike New York City living it was with its big, high-ceilinged rooms leading out to lavish gardens, and the enormous swimming-pool. The sun was shining and music was playing in the background. It was the radio, because every so often a male disc jockey would announce his last three choices. She remembered the dogs, yappy little things racing all over the place.

"They're my babies," Salli had said, scooping them up

in her arms. And then, later, Salli had confided that she couldn't have kids – something to do with an abortion that had taken place when she was fifteen. "I was dirt poor," she'd said, with a rueful laugh, "so I guess I got me the town butcher."

"Is that off the record, or can I use it?" Madison had asked, playing fair because she didn't want to take advantage of Salli's almost childlike openness.

"Go ahead – print the truth for once," Salli had answered boldly. "I'm sick of all the lies." And then she'd *really* started talking.

Good journalist that she was, Madison had made short-hand notes in her head as Salli rambled on, even though her machine was recording every word, because nowadays the lawyers wouldn't allow the magazine to print an interview unless there was tape to back it up.

Sitting beside the pool, chewing on carrot sticks because she was on a constant diet, Salli began peeling back the layers of her life.

*

Small-town girl Salli got pregnant, had an abortion, won a local beauty contest at the age of fifteen, fought with her widowed father, dropped out of school and took the bus to Hollywood with exactly one hundred and three dollars in her cracked white patent-leather purse. She had brown frizzy hair, slightly buck teeth and quite a bit of puppy fat. But she was still pretty enough to make heads turn.

She faked her ID and immediately got a job as a waitress in a strip joint out by LAX airport, where she was so impressed by most of the strippers' attributes that she decided she'd better do something about her own modest 34Bs. With that goal in mind she began to save her money.

While she was waiting, a cab-driver boyfriend took a nude Polaroid of her and sent it in to *Playboy*. Eight weeks later they rejected her as too skinny. This infuriated Salli, who immediately became determined that one day she'd be on the magazine's cover.

New tits became more important than ever. She found herself an agent and started doing extra work. Naturally, the agent, an older man with grown kids, fell in lust with her. Of course, he had no clue that she was barely sixteen. She held out against going to bed with him until he came up with the money for her new boobs. It took a year because, being a nice family man, he was riddled with guilt. Eventually he left his wife, paid for her operation and, on the night they finally slept together, expired on top of her before consummating the act. It was a traumatic experience, which Salli did not forget in a hurry.

After that she became an expert tease, never letting any man get too close, although they all tried. Instead she concentrated on making herself the best she could be.

The new boobs gave her a head start: they changed her life. Instead of waitressing she turned to exotic dancing and began making enough money to continue her transformation from small-town beauty queen to Hollywood starlet. First she dyed her brown hair a Marilyn Monroe platinum blonde. Then she had her teeth capped, and managed to lose a staggering twenty-five pounds. With her new glamorous look – all big boobs, tiny waist and long legs –

she soon found another agent and began getting small roles on TV shows and in films. If she'd wanted to do porno she could've made a killing, but sensibly she opted not to go that route. Instead, she specialized in playing dumb blondes with spectacular bodies. An easy task. What wasn't so easy was fighting off all the men. They came on to her in droves – including married famous ones who all had the same excuse: "My wife isn't into sex, so suck my dick." Sometimes she did, sometimes she didn't. She had to like a guy before she did anything.

It was a long haul, but Salli finally made it back to *Playboy*. This time they were all over her, and not only did she get the cover, but four pages of photographs inside *and* the centrefold.

Fame at last. Her spread was so popular that a year later she did it again. And then her career really started to take off, culminating in her own TV series, *Teach!*, and yet another *Playboy* cover.

Teach! became the *Baywatch* of the nineties, and Salli became the heroine of horny teenage boys across the world.

Along the way she married an actor, Eddie Stoner, divorced him two years later. And was currently married to the infamous Bobby Skorch – a man who regularly risked his life for a living.

*

Once more Madison wondered what had happened after she'd left. Salli had seemed in such a good mood, upbeat and enthusiastic about her future. She'd told Madison she planned to stay on *Teach!* for one more year, and then take a shot at movie stardom.

Now it was all over. And there had to be a reason why.

Madison drove on determinedly towards Salli's house.

L.A.
Connections
2

CHAPTER THIRTEEN

"I DON'T BELIEVE this," Max said, enraged.

"Howdy, pal," Howie said, oblivious to his friend's anger. "I want you to meet Inga."

Max glared furiously at the exquisite supermodel lounging casually on the leather banquette in a barely there black dress. "What the fuck are *you* doing here?" he exploded.

"You two know each other?" Howie asked, obviously surprised.

"Not only do we know each other," Max blustered, "but Inga was my date tonight, and she failed to show."

"Don't be so silly, Max," Inga said, in her infuriatingly precise accent. "I was *not* your date. We had a business appointment I could not make. And kindly do not use foul language."

Max's famous smoothness slid away as his face contorted

71

with frustrated rage. This Swedish bitch was dissing *him*, Max Steele. No fucking way. And what the hell was she doing with a low-life like Howie, his supposed friend?

"Am I in the middle of something here?" Howie asked, all playboy innocence.

"Not at all," Inga answered coolly.

"Did we, or did we not, have an appointment?" Max demanded, dropping the word date.

"A vague arrangement, nothing definite," Inga said, dipping two fingers into her champagne glass, then licking them delicately in a highly suggestive way.

"Hey," Howie said, sliding out of the booth, "I'll be in the head if anyone needs me."

Max sat down on the leather banquette. "Inga," he said, regaining his composure, "you were supposed to meet me at Freddie Leon's house, remember? It was an important sit-down dinner and it was place-carded. Your absence was embarrassing – not to mention rude. You can't get away with shit like that in this town and expect to work." He glared at her, waiting for a reaction. "Do you understand me?"

Inga regarded him for a long, silent moment. "Inga does what Inga wants," she said, at last. "And I can assure you, Max, that when the right project comes along, they will be begging Inga to appear."

Max was stunned. Just who did this broad think she was? "Honey," he said, "keep on believing *that*, and you can watch your movie career *never* take flight." Abruptly he got up from the table. "I'm off the case – find yourself a new agent."

Howie was in the men's room snorting a line of coke from the dark green marble counter-top. The attendant, having been handed a fifty-dollar tip, was looking the other way.

"You're lucky I'm not undercover Vice," Max said, stealing a healthy pinch of the white powder and rubbing it into his gums.

"They'd never get in the door," Howie said with a manic chuckle. "This place is protected."

"Protected my ass," Max snapped.

Howie slipped the small plastic straw into his pocket and wiped the tip of his nose, getting rid of any tell-tale white powder. "What's with you and the babe?" he said. "She really break a date with you?"

"Nobody breaks a date with Max Steele," Max said stiffly. "It was purely business, and the stupid bitch blew it."

"*I've* got something I'd like her to blow," Howie chortled, grabbing his crotch in an exaggerated manner.

"Where'd you meet her?" Max asked, still fuming but hiding it well.

"Cocktail party at Cartier's earlier. She was standing there looking hot, so I bought her a trinket."

"Trinket?" Max questioned.

Howie laughed sheepishly. "So it was a gold tank watch. Big deal. It got me a date, an' you gotta admit – she's the business. Makes Cindy look plain."

"Models *are* better-looking than actresses," Max admitted, feeling better as the coke began to take effect. "Although, you gotta remember, they're also stupider."

Howie gave a ribald laugh. "I wanna fuck her, not take a lesson in physics."

"I heard a rumour she's got the clap," Max said, his mean streak surfacing.

"No shit?" Howie said, too stoned to care.

By the time they returned to the booth, Inga was gone. "She must be in the john," Howie said.

With a deep sense of satisfaction Max knew better. She'd dumped on Howie just as she'd dumped on him.

Supermodels. Tall and tan and young and dumb. He'd know better than to chase after one of *them* again.

L.A. Connections 2

CHAPTER FOURTEEN

"WHY DID we have to leave?" Kevin whined, as Angie raced his black Ferrari recklessly along Sunset. "I was havin' fun."

"If that's your idea of fun," Angie sneered, "then you, like, need *major* detox."

"Fuck you!"

"Fuck you, too!" she retorted, screeching the powerful car to a halt at a stop light. "I'm not into all that phony BS. If you weren't a friggin' movie star, those people wouldn't talk to you."

"So?" Kevin said belligerently. "I *am* a friggin' movie star."

"You're not Leonardo DiCaprio."

"Wouldn't want t'be," Kevin said sulkily, thinking that it was about time he dumped her. She was too bossy by far, and now that he had two big box-office successes behind him, he could get any girl he wanted. Angie didn't know it but she was busy nagging herself out of a gig. "Where we goin'?" he asked, noticing that she'd zoomed past the street where they'd set up house together.

"I need to score," she said, rubbing her forehead. "I'm, like, totally bummed."

You need to clean up your act, he thought. Angie was heavily into drugs and he wasn't. Been there. Done that. He had no desire to become the next Robert Downey Jr or Charlie Sheen. Those guys were old enough to know better.

"Fuck," he mumbled. "I can't go scorin' drugs with you. It's not good for my image."

"You never do anything for me," she complained.

"It's time you dropped out of the drug scene," he said, thinking about Lucinda Bennett and the movie they were going to make together.

"I don't need a freakin' lecture," Angie snapped. "I just lost a very close friend."

"I never heard you mention Salli."

"That's 'cause we had a big fight before you and I got together."

"Big fight about what?"

"When I was sixteen we used to share an apartment," Angie said. "Until she stole my boyfriend who wasn't even worth stealing. He was a son-of-a-bitch. I bet it was *him* who killed her."

"What're you talking about *now*?"

"Eddie Stoner."

"Eddie Stoner," Kevin repeated. "The actor?"

"You know him?"

"Think I worked with him once."

"Did you or didn't you?"

"Who remembers?"

"Anyway – he was a rough bastard, so I figured if Salli wanted him so much she could have him. I moved out, and a couple of weeks later she and Eddie got married in Vegas." Angie sighed her disgust. "Some *dumb* move. All he had going for him was a big dick and a sharp right hand. He used to beat the shit out of me, and as soon as they were married he started on her. I thought, 'cause she was older than me, she'd be able to handle him. But she couldn't. One night she phoned me, and she was hysterical. I told her, 'Don't come cryin' to me – you wanted the loser, you got him.' And I didn't help her. Then she started to get famous and all that shit. Eventually she divorced him. It was a real drag. I know she had to call the cops on him a few times, and that he threatened to kill her. Hey, he threatened to kill *me* when we were together. I'm surprised he didn't come creeping back when *I* made it, considering *I* made it bigger than *her*." She paused, then added thoughtfully, "Maybe I should tell the cops what I know."

"You can't go around accusing people," Kevin said, frowning. "You want us *both* dragged through the tabloids?"

"Okay, Kev," Angela said, her mind on other matters. "Let me score a gram or two an' I'll think it over."

"You gotta get out of the drug scene," Kevin repeated sternly.

"I can," she answered defiantly. "Any time I want."

"Sure."

"Yeah, *sure.*"

"You're difficult, Angie, you never listen."

"I know, you've told me a million times. But what would you do without me, Kev? You'd be running around this town with your dick in your hand, and they'd all be taking you for the ride of the century. Right?"

"If you say so." And he wondered exactly how he should go about dumping her.

L.A.
Connections
2

CHAPTER FIFTEEN

DETECTIVE TUCCI called his wife, Faye, and told her that, just as he'd expected, the area around Salli T. Turner's house was turning into a media circus. There were TV trucks with their news crews, reporters, and crowds of people milling around outside on the street. Everyone was contained behind police lines while helicopters hovered overhead, and in the house the phone did not stop ringing. Even though it was late at night, word had spread fast.

Detective Tucci swore softly under his breath. There would definitely be no dinner tonight, not unless it was take-out pizza, and he hated to do that to his stomach.

By midnight the police photographer had finished his grisly task, and the medical examiner was now in charge. Later Salli's mutilated body was put on a stretcher and taken off in an ambulance headed for the morgue where an autopsy would take place and evidence would be gathered.

When the ambulance attendants loaded it aboard, the crowds went wild, screaming and yelling her name. Detective Tucci couldn't help wondering if the murderer was out there somewhere, watching . . . waiting . . . getting his kicks.

The facts, as Detective Tucci knew them, were as such: there was no sign of a break-in, which meant that Salli had obviously known her killer and had probably let him into the house. She must have been comfortable with him – if, indeed, it was a male – because she'd taken him into the living room and out by the pool. In the sink behind the bar Detective Tucci had found two hastily washed glasses. He'd immediately put them into a plastic bag and sent them to the lab to be checked.

So, he decided, whoever the killer was had entered through the front door, Salli had greeted them, they'd had a drink together, walked out near the patio, and then, for some unknown reason, he or she had worked themselves into a frenzy and stabbed her to death.

The houseman had probably been on his way to see what all the noise was about because, according to neighbours, music had been playing loudly and the dogs were barking non-stop. On his way, Froo, the Asian houseman, had encountered the killer, who'd shot him point-blank in the face, which indicated that Froo would have recognized the man – or woman.

For the last two hours Detective Tucci had been trying to contact Salli's husband, Bobby Skorch. Apparently he was in a car somewhere on his way back from a gig in Vegas.

His cellphone was turned off, and he appeared to be unreachable.

Detective Tucci wondered if Bobby had murdered his wife. It wouldn't be the first time a husband was responsible. Maybe he had driven back early from his appearance, fought with Salli, stabbed her to death, then got back in his car, driven away and would turn up later – the distraught husband. It was hardly an uncommon scenario.

He sat at a table in the kitchen making numerous notes. He was known for his detailed accounts and he enjoyed making sure that he didn't miss one single thing.

Somewhere in this puzzle there was an answer, and he fully intended to find out what it was.

L.A.
Connections
2

CHAPTER SIXTEEN

MADISON PARKED a couple of blocks from the house. There were TV camera crews and reporters everywhere, and, of course, huge crowds of onlookers. The police had already roped off the area around the house and there was a strangely festive atmosphere, as if people were revelling in the action.

She left her car and hurried over to the nearest cop. "Who's the detective in charge of this case?" she asked, flashing her press pass.

"Can't give out any information at this moment," the cop said, barely glancing at her.

"I understand that," she said evenly. "However, I know he'll want to talk to me, so please would you get a message to him. My name's Madison Castelli, I'm a journalist from New York and I spent the day with Ms Turner in her house."

"Really?" the cop said disbelievingly.

"Yes, really," Madison replied.

"Can you prove that?"

"How am I supposed to prove it?"

"With all due respect, ma'am, there are a lot of people here trying to get into the house . . ."

"I'm sure there are, but if you tell the detective that I was with her today, I'm certain he'll want to see me."

"I told you, ma'am, I can't do that, there's too much going on."

"Look," Madison said, fast losing patience, "I work for *Manhattan Style*, my editor is Victor Simons." She handed him a card. "This is his number. If you give this to the detective in charge, he can check with my editor and verify my story. Other than that I don't know what I can do, but I *do* know that he'll want to see me."

"Not tonight, ma'am. Maybe he'll interview you tomorrow. Why don't you leave your name and number and go on home?"

"Can I be sure he'll get it?" she said, swallowing her annoyance because she knew it wouldn't do any good to lose her temper.

"Absolutely, ma'am."

"At my house I have an audiotape of Salli. On it she talks about everything that's going on in her life. I'm sure it will be helpful."

The cop took another look at her. Maybe she wasn't handing him a bullshit story. Maybe she was legit. "Why'n't you wait here a minute?" he said. "I'll go check."

"Thanks."

She watched as the cop made his way into the house. Where were Natalie and Jimmy? They should be here already. She could see quite a few on-the-scene reporters standing on the street doing remotes to their TV stations.

After a few minutes the cop returned. "Detective Tucci says he'll be in touch tomorrow."

"Are you telling me he doesn't want to see me now?"

"That's right, ma'am."

"Then I guess I'll write the story my way, and mention that the detective on the case refused to see me. I'm sure the *L.A. Times* will be interested in a first-hand account."

"Whatever you say, ma'am."

"I'm merely telling you what I plan to do, so you can pass it on to Detective Tucci."

"I'll let him know."

She returned to her rented car, drove to the nearest gas station, went into the phone booth, and looked up Tucci in the phone book. Then she started making calls. Third time lucky.

"Is Detective Tucci there?" she asked the woman who answered.

"I'm sorry, he's not."

"Is this his wife?"

"Yes. Can I help you?"

"It's most important that I speak to your husband. I have information pertaining to the case he's working on. I talked to an officer in charge of crowd control, and I'm not sure if he gave Detective Tucci my message. I work for *Manhattan Style* magazine."

"Oh, I know that magazine," Faye interrupted. "I read it every month."

"Glad to hear it. Then you might know me – Madison Castelli?"

"Certainly, Miss Castelli, I've read your work. I like it a lot."

"Call me Madison. And your name is?"

"Faye."

"Okay, Faye – well, um . . . tell your husband I had lunch with Salli today, I have an audiotape of our interview, and I'd really like to see him personally."

"Oh, I'll do that," Faye said, impressed. "You can depend on me."

Madison gave Faye her phone number, then, secure in the knowledge that she'd done her duty, she got in her car and drove back to Natalie's.

Cole, Natalie's brother, was sprawled on the couch in front of the TV, staring at the screen. "You heard the news?" he said, as she walked in.

"Yes."

"I used to train Salli, y'know."

"You did?"

"Yeah, a coupla years ago, when she was married to her first husband, Eddie. He was a maniac. She was a peach."

Madison sat down on the edge of the couch. "Tell me about him."

"Salli used to tell me stuff," Cole said. "To everybody else she'd say she got a black eye or all beat up walking into a door. One time he broke her arm and I had to rush her to the hospital. She called the cops on him a coupla times, but he'd always talk them round. She was lucky to get away from him."

"Are you saying you think he did it?"

"Wouldn't be surprised," Cole said, with a shrug. "He had a way hot temper. That dude was *always* pissed about something."

"Like what?"

"You know the deal. He was a small-time actor – worked plenty but was never the star. This made him *real* sour. I stopped working out with her when Eddie began getting jealous."

"Of you?"

"Yeah."

"But you're gay."

Cole laughed mirthlessly. "Try telling Eddie. He didn't want her around *any* guy who looked good. He was into control, that's *all* he wanted. I'm kinda surprised she got away from him. It took a lot of strength."

"What was his name again?"

"Eddie Stoner," Cole said grimly.

Madison got up and went to her laptop, where she put in a request to New York for information.

Eddie Stoner. Let's find out exactly who you are.

L.A.
Connections
2

CHAPTER SEVENTEEN

"OH . . . MY . . . God," Kristin murmured, stretching luxuriously. "That was pretty . . . damn . . . good."

Jake pinned her arms above her head, holding her wrists tightly so she could barely move. "That wasn't pretty damn good," he said sternly. "That was sensational, and you know it."

"Yes, of course I know it," she said, giggling softly. "You don't have to torture me to make me talk."

"And what makes you think I'm about to torture you?" he asked, mock-serious.

"I don't know. Maybe you'll make love to me again."

"Would that be torture?"

"Oh, yes. Beautiful, incredible, fantastic torture."

He laughed. "I guess I'm going to have to make you beg."

"Really?" she said, attempting to roll out from under him.

"Yup," he said decisively. "I'm gonna have to do it."

"Okay, how do I beg?" she said, realizing she'd never felt so relaxed and carefree and happy as she did at that very moment.

"You say, 'Please, Jake.'"

"Please, Jake," she repeated, unable to keep the laughter out of her voice.

"Now say, 'I beg you, Jake, to give me more.'"

"I'm not saying that."

"Don't argue. I'm trying to teach you."

"Dear Jake," she said, smiling. "That was so damn good that I'm *begging* you for more."

He bent his head to her left nipple, teasing it with his tongue. "Keep begging," he said. "I like it."

She felt his hardness against her naked thigh, and sighed with pleasure. "Isn't it time you begged me?" she suggested, after a few moments of utter bliss.

"Huh?"

"I want to hear *you* beg."

"You do?"

"Right now, soldier!"

"Hey!" A big smile spread across his face. "This is like we've been together for years."

She laughed softly. "Well, we haven't."

"Oh, *big* surprise," he said jokingly. "But we're going to be – right?"

Why did he have to spoil everything? "Jake," she said,

searching for the right words, "I haven't been completely honest with you."

"Don't want to hear about it now. You can be completely honest with me over lunch tomorrow. But right now, let's just enjoy the moment."

She tried to roll away again. He turned her back toward him and began sucking her lower lip. "I never realized," she gasped, "that kissing could be so erotic."

"Then you've got a lot of learning to do."

"Will you teach me, Jake?"

"You want me to?"

"Yes."

"Well, first you've got to gently caress the lips with your tongue very, very slowly. Like this."

"Oh, you're good," she said, shivering.

"So I've been told," he answered, confidently.

"And who told you?"

"Huh?"

"Well, you informed me you hadn't been with a woman for over a year," she said curiously. "So who told you?"

A long pause before he spoke. "My wife," he said, at last. "She died in a car crash a year ago."

"Oh, God, I'm sorry – I didn't know."

"You know the old cliché – there's nothing like time to heal. Anyway, we were separated when it happened."

"Were you getting a divorce?"

"She was seeing another guy. In fact, she was on her way to visit him when a truck came out of a side street and totalled her car. She had no chance."

"Are you telling me she left you for someone else?"

"Yup, that's exactly right. Which is why there hasn't been anyone since. Because how could I trust anyone after that? Megan was my high-school sweetheart, we were married straight out of school. I thought we had a pretty good marriage, and then . . ." He trailed off.

"Jake, I . . . I'm really sorry."

"When somebody lets you down it's difficult to trust again. But then I saw you sitting in Neiman Marcus, and you had this great luminous quality, and I *knew* you were special. And now, days later, here we are. God works in mysterious ways, huh?"

She was suffused with guilt. Why did this have to happen? Why did she have to fall in love with a man to whom she could never tell the truth? And how was she going to extract herself from this situation? Because there was absolutely no way she could ever tell him.

"Hey," Jake said, "this wasn't supposed to turn into a confessional. This is you and me starting out, it's not about either of our pasts. But while we're on the subject, is there anything you want to tell me?"

Plenty, she thought, suffused with guilt. *But there's no way I'm going to.*

She put her arms around him to hide her shame, and hugged him very tight. She was definitely going to make this a night to remember . . . because after this one night of passion, she'd decided she would never see him again.

"So," Jake said, smiling, "what did I do to deserve such affection?"

"Everything," she murmured.

And then he was kissing her again. And before she knew it they were making love for the second time. And it was so amazing, so different, so satisfying.

And just as she was heading towards another great climax, the phone rang, jangling her back to reality.

"Ignore it," Jake said, still inside her, pinning her beneath his body, the feel of him driving her crazy.

She wondered who it could be, but she didn't have to wonder long because after three rings her answering-machine picked up.

Oh, God, she thought, panic-stricken. *I forgot to turn the damn machine off.*

Jake was also close to a climax, so there was no way she could escape to turn down the volume.

"Hi, Kristin, sweetie," said Darlene. "Boy, has Mr X got a hot nut for *you*. Talk about obsession. Can you believe he wants to book you again tonight, and he's willing to spring for another five thousand big ones for the privilege? Twice in one night. Honey, you've really got it going." A husky giggle. "What's your secret? A mink-lined snatch? Call me back ASAP. The man is waiting."

L.A.
Connections
2

CHAPTER EIGHTEEN

MADISON AWOKE to Natalie pushing her shoulder. "What's up?" she mumbled.

"There's a Detective Tucci on the phone," Natalie said, already dressed and made up. "Isn't he the detective covering the Salli T. Turner case?"

"That's right," Madison answered, suppressing a yawn.

"Why's he calling you?" Natalie asked curiously.

"Because I phoned his house last night. I couldn't get into the location and I thought I should talk to him about the audio-tape I have of Salli." Leaning over, she reached for the phone. "This is Madison Castelli."

"Miss Castelli," Detective Tucci said, his tone slow and measured, "I understand you have some information for me."

"Yes, I do. You see, I was with Salli yesterday. She gave

me an in-depth interview for my magazine. In fact, I have the tape if you'd be interested in hearing it."

"Most definitely."

"Shall I come to the station?"

"That's very accommodating of you, Miss Castelli, but I'll be at the Pacific Palisades house all morning. Can you come there?"

"Certainly."

"I'll expect you as soon as possible."

Madison replaced the receiver. "There goes Freddie Leon for the day," she said wryly.

Natalie handed her a well-needed cup of coffee. "What do you mean?"

"If I'm going to meet the detective, how can I get into Freddie today? I was planning on dropping by the IAA office to visit Max Steele."

"You couldn't anyway," Natalie pointed out. "It's Sunday, they'd be closed."

"Oh, right."

"And regarding Max Steele," Natalie added, "there's a story about him in the *Times*. Seems he's leaving IAA to head up Orpheus Studios."

"You're kidding?"

"It's on the second page."

"Really?"

"Is this a surprise?"

"He told me he had some news, only I didn't realize it was going to be public knowledge so fast. I'd better call him."

"He's probably sleeping."

Madison reached for her robe and got out of bed. "What happened after I left last night?"

"Oh, Garth was his usual uncharming self," Natalie said. "I was at the station all night interviewing anybody who knew Salli, and putting together a retrospective. It's media-frenzy time, all anybody's talking about. And once they find out you were with her, *you*'ll be a media sensation, too."

"Thanks a lot," Madison said drily. "If you hadn't told your news director—"

"What can *he* do?"

"Tell other people, to punish me for not appearing on his shitty show."

"It's not a shitty show," Natalie said defensively.

"Sorry, I didn't mean that."

"Yes, you did!"

Madison felt bad about insulting her friend. "C'mon, Nat," she said warmly, "let's not start the day off badly. Did they reach Salli's husband yet?"

"Yeah, there's coverage of him going into the house looking wrecked."

"What about the ex, Eddie Stoner? Have they questioned him?"

"They're looking. Nobody seems to know where he's at."

"Is he the prime suspect?"

"Could be. God!" Natalie exclaimed. "Can you imagine what the tabloids are going to do with this story?"

Madison nodded. "It'll turn into another OJ and Nicole circus."

"You got it," Natalie said. "Only this time they won't be able to play the race card. Thank God!"

"No, but you can bet they'll play the sex card," Madison said. "You know, sexy blonde, big boobs, all of that sexist crap – like Salli was asking for it."

"You think so?"

"I *know* so. She was beautiful, rich, sexy *and* a woman. Major strike against getting any kind of fair treatment." Madison sighed. "This whole thing makes me sick. Yesterday she was alive, today she's dead. I simply can't believe it."

"Me neither," said Cole, walking into the room. "I heard on Channel Five that Salli's dad's flying in from Chicago, and there's a private funeral tomorrow. I'd like to be there."

"That's a tough one," Natalie said. "Salli had so many fans – they'll all want to be there."

"I'd still like to go," Cole said.

"Me, too," Madison agreed. "How can we arrange it?"

"I'll see what I can find out," Natalie said. "Right now I've got to get back to the studio. Then Luther wants to take me to lunch and, girl, I am *not* passing *him* up."

As soon as Natalie left, Madison decided to call Max Steele. She had his home number, so she picked up the phone and got through immediately. "Hi, Max," she said. "This is Madison – remember? Breakfast yesterday?"

He sounded groggy. "What's doin'?"

"I read your news."

"News?"

"You told me you had an announcement, but you didn't tell me it was going to appear today."

"What announcement?" Max said, kicking off his bed-covers, realizing he was suffering from a monster hangover.

"Is it true you're taking over Ariel Shore's job at Orpheus?"

"Shit!" he said, sitting up. "Where'd you hear that?"

"It's in the *Times*."

"Christ!" he said. And he knew what had happened. Freddie had opened the door before he was ready to leave, and shoved him out. Hard. Now Billy Cornelius would be mad as hell, and there was nothing he could do about it.

"Off the record," Madison said, "would you mind giving me Freddie Leon's home number?"

"Why?" Max asked suspiciously. "You wanna talk to him about this?"

"No, it has nothing to do with you. I'm simply looking to find out everything I can about him. That *is* why I'm out here."

"If you want the dirt on Freddie, talk to his secretary, Ria Santiago. She knows things nobody else does."

"Would you happen to have *her* phone number?"

"Yeah, I'll give you both numbers." *Nothing like a little sweet revenge*, Max thought.

Madison hung up and glanced at her watch. It was too early to call anyone else: waking Max was one thing but she figured she'd be nice and let the others sleep for an hour or so, although she was sure Freddie Leon was an early riser – he looked the type.

While she was waiting she called Victor in New York, where it was three hours later. "I'm holding the press for your story," Victor said. "I need it like yesterday."

"I'm seeing the detective on the case this morning. As soon as I get back I'll write it up and fax it to you."

"Good," Victor said. "And maybe you can include the name of the killer."

"Yeah, sure, Victor," she drawled. "Why not? Simple."

"No need to be sarcastic, Maddy. I'll talk to you later."

"Yes, Victor, later."

CHAPTER NINETEEN

ARIEL SHORE arrived at Billy Cornelius's house at eight in the morning and insisted upon seeing him. Ethel, his feisty wife, was still asleep. The butler, a prudent man, did not wake her. Instead he ushered Ariel into the living room, where she waited impatiently for ten long minutes.

When Billy finally appeared, she thrust the *L.A. Times* in his face. "What's *this*?" she said, through clenched teeth, towering over him.

Billy Cornelius stared bad-temperedly at the newspaper. "What're you talking about?" he snapped, his left eye twitching.

"This ridiculous story about Max Steele getting my job," Ariel said. "Read it."

Billy scanned the story with beady, red-rimmed eyes. "Bullpuddy, hogwash," he said.

"It better be," Ariel said sternly. "Because I'm sure you wouldn't relish Ethel finding out about us."

Billy curled his lip. "You wouldn't do that, Ariel."

"Think again, Billy. I certainly would."

"You promised."

"I *know* what I promised," she said, marching up and down. "And I know what *you* promised. You break yours, I can break mine. What is this crap with Max Steele anyway?"

"I was planning on telling you," Billy said. "I considered bringing him in as head of production. Nothing definite."

She arched a disgusted eyebrow. "Without informing me?"

"Max is a go-getter, he knows everyone."

Ariel planted herself in front of her so-called boss. "Listen to me, Billy, and listen carefully. *I* run the studio. You do not make decisions like that without my input. Max Steele will have nothing to do with Orpheus. *Nothing.* Is that perfectly clear? Because if it's not, I'm sure that Ethel will be able to make it *very* clear to you."

"You have nothing to worry about," Billy said, backing down in the face of Ariel's fury.

"And next time you sneak around behind my back," Ariel said, eyes glittering dangerously, "you'd better be more careful. I want a retraction, and I want to see it in Monday morning's paper. Do we understand each other, Billy?"

Billy Cornelius nodded. He might be one of the richest men in America, but when Ariel Shore screamed, he jumped.

CHAPTER TWENTY

WHEN DIANA awoke on Sunday morning she realized that Freddie had not returned home the night before. It wasn't the first time he'd stayed out all night.

Nevertheless she was livid. How dare he think he could simply walk out and not return?

And where exactly was he? Not that she was worried about other women – Freddie had never been a sexual being. Even at the beginning of their marriage they'd made love infrequently; then, several years ago, their lovemaking had stopped altogether.

No, it wasn't another woman. It was Freddie's way of hurting her. First he ruined her dinner party, then he stayed out all night. What a cold bastard he could be.

The children were away in Connecticut, staying with her mother, so the house was quite peaceful. She got out of bed and marched downstairs to the kitchen. The caterers had done a masterful job of cleaning up.

Throwing open the fridge she surveyed the leftovers, wrapped neatly in Saran Wrap. Cold hors d'oeuvres always appealed to her, so she took out an egg roll and wolfed it down without thinking. Then she stomped around the house, making sure everything was in place and that the catering staff hadn't stolen anything. Diana lived in fear that someone was going to rip her off. It could be because she had been brought up by extremely strict parents in Utah, who suspected everyone of stealing. She'd never forgotten her stern upbringing.

The Sunday *L.A. Times* was neatly laid out on the kitchen table, alongside the *New York Times*. Usually Freddie got to them first; he was fastidious about his newspapers and did not like anyone else touching them before him. However, today Diana felt it was her duty to mess them up before he got home.

The heading of a story on page two caught her attention.

ARIEL OUT, MAX IN.
MAX STEELE TO LEAVE IAA AND
JOIN ORPHEUS

How could this possibly have gotten into the newspapers so quickly? Somebody must have leaked it early, long before Freddie and Max's confrontation.

Diana read the story quickly, then rushed to the phone.

Max answered immediately. "Yes?" he snapped, sounding most unfriendly.

"Max, this is Diana. Can we meet?"

"Why?" he asked suspiciously.

"There's something I wish to discuss."

"Is it about Freddie?"

"He mustn't know we're meeting."

"Whatever you say, Diana."

"Nine thirty at the Four Seasons. The dining room."

"I'll be there," Max said.

"Good," Diana replied. She'd known he wouldn't turn her down.

L.A.
Connections
2

CHAPTER TWENTY-ONE

EDDIE STONER was awakened from a liquor-induced sleep at six a.m. on Sunday morning by two burly cops, who burst rudely into his apartment and informed him he was under arrest. He was between girlfriends at the time, so there was no one to buffer their entrance.

"What the fuck is this about?" Eddie mumbled, as they instructed him to get out of bed.

"Parking tickets," cop number one said. "You got thirty-four of 'em, all unpaid. You're under arrest, bud, so let's go."

"Parking tickets!" Eddie Stoner said, throwing off the sheet, knowing he was naked and not caring. Let the cops get an eyeful and see what they didn't have.

"Yeah, unpaid tickets," said cop number two, proceeding to read him his rights.

"Jesus Christ!" Eddie grumbled, reaching for his pants. "Don't you guys have anythin' better t' do?"

"Where'd you get that scratch on your chest?" cop number one asked.

"Didn't realize gettin' a parkin' ticket meant havin' to explain my physical state," Eddie replied, running a hand through his mane of dirty blond hair. "There's one on my ass, too – wanna take a peek? My girlfriend's got long fingernails."

"Get dressed," cop number two said.

Eddie Stoner shrugged, threw on a T-shirt and some sneakers. "Fuck!" he said. "You're haulin' me in for parkin' tickets. Who the fuck'd believe *this*?"

L.A.
Connections
2

CHAPTER TWENTY-TWO

MADISON PLAYED the tape as she drove her rented car to Salli's house. It was truly heartbreaking to hear Salli explain her life in her own words, exactly as Madison remembered. She found it particularly interesting when Salli talked about Eddie Stoner. "Eddie was basically a good guy," Salli said. "Just frustrated 'cause, like, his mom drove him loco. Never left him alone for a moment, laid a big fat guilt trip on him 'cause his father ran out on them when Eddie was twelve. So, like, he always felt kind of responsible for her. An' she got off on that – telling him he was a bum and no good. Guess he wanted to prove her right. She hated me, thought I was a little tramp. Said so to my face. Well, I guess I gotta confess – Eddie did beat me up a few times. But it wasn't his fault, and later he was always so nice and loving, begging my forgiveness. I had to escape, though. Otherwise he would've dragged me down with him."

Madison listened to her own voice on the tape. "If I remember correctly, Salli, you told me on the plane that Eddie was a psycho, freakazoid, asshole actor who sued *you* for alimony. You also told me that he thinks one day you'll take him back."

"Wow!" Salli's voice again. "*You*'ve got a good memory."

"So which is it? Was he a sweetheart? Or a wife-beater?"

"A little bit of both," Salli said. And then, wistfully, "But I must've loved him at one time."

Madison switched off the tape. She wished she'd asked more questions about Eddie Stoner.

Now it was too late.

*

"Nice of you to come, Miss Castelli," Detective Tucci said, greeting her at the door. He was a tall, heavy-set man with brown hair and faded blue eyes. Not unattractive, Madison thought, as he took her arm and led her inside the house. Walking through the hall without Salli there to greet her felt strange. Automatically, she glanced up at the giant portrait. It was still there, smiling down at everybody.

"Merely doing my duty," she replied. "When I leave here I'm writing a piece for my magazine, and I thought I should let you know what I have, in case it could be useful for your investigation."

"That's very thoughtful of you, Miss Castelli."

"On the tape Salli talks about her ex-husband, Eddie

Stoner. When we flew into L.A. a couple of days ago she was telling me he always expected they'd get back together. Do you think he could've—?"

"Mr Stoner's already in custody on parking-ticket violations," Detective Tucci said. "Of course, that's official information, not for publication. I can trust you, Miss Castelli, can't I?"

"Please call me Madison," she said, nodding. "I spoke to your wife, she was most charming on the phone."

"Faye's a good woman."

"Salli was a terrific girl," Madison said. "You've only seen the public image, but to know her was to realize that she had a certain sweetness that really came through. I'm so saddened by this horrible tragedy."

"The world seems to be," Detective Tucci said. "There's already several websites set up to discuss her murder."

"I can imagine."

"May I listen to the tape back in my office?" Detective Tucci said. "Then maybe I can ask you questions about it later."

"I made a copy for you."

"You're very organized."

"I'm a good journalist."

"My wife said that. She speaks very highly of your work. Faye's the one who has the time to read magazines. I don't."

Madison laughed politely.

"Are you from here?" he asked.

"New York," Madison said. "I'm in L.A. preparing a story on Freddie Leon."

"I'm afraid I don't know who that is."

JACKIE COLLINS

"Your wife would, I'm sure."

"Oh, yes, Faye – she knows all about show-business." Madison smiled again. She liked this man: he was warm and seemed to care. "Did you meet the houseman yesterday?" Detective Tucci asked.

"Froo. Yes, I did. I gather he's the other victim."

"We think he heard noises and came to investigate."

"Well, Detective, if there's anything I can do, please don't hesitate to call me."

"You say she had a certain sweetness?"

"That's right."

"I'd like to solve this one."

"Tell me, do you think it could be the ex-husband?"

Detective Tucci shook his head. "I never make random guesses. With DNA today we'll be able to find out in no time."

"Just like they did with Nicole Simpson, right?" Madison said, unable to resist the dig.

"That was a botched case."

"I'm sure you won't botch this one. I trust that you'll do Salli justice."

"It's my intention, Miss Castelli. It's certainly my intention."

112

L.A.
Connections
2

CHAPTER TWENTY-THREE

MAX COULD not believe what was happening to him. One moment he was a partner in the most successful talent agency in Los Angeles, the next he was about to head up a studio, and now Billy Cornelius had just got off the phone, telling him that things had changed and there was no way they could work together.

"What do you mean 'changed'?" Max had blustered.

"You should never have leaked it," Billy had said. "Too late now. The deal's off."

Max was furious. Now he'd have to go crawling back to Freddie and say, "Let's forgive and forget." Only Freddie was not the forgiving kind. Everyone knew that.

Max couldn't help thinking about Inga Cruelle. He'd always had great success with women: how dare she treat him like he was simply another guy on the make?

113

He glanced at his gold Rolex, it was almost time to meet Diana. Before he did, however, there was something he had to do. He had a plan.

He went to the phone and called Kristin. To his annoyance her answering machine picked up.

"Hey, baby," he said. "This is Max Steele. I've made a decision. I'm taking you out of the business, honey. Making you exclusive. You tell me what it'll cost to set you up, and I'll do it." He paused for a moment, quite pleased with himself. "I've been thinking about things. I want you to be with me. Y'see, I need somebody like you around, somebody to keep me focused. I can introduce you to people, change your life. Nobody'll know who you are, or what you used to be. This is gonna work out, Kristin." Another pause. "I have a meeting at eleven, so call me any time after twelve an' we'll work something out. Okay, honey?"

And when he hung up he was convinced he had her. Beautiful Kristin beside him would change his luck.

*

Diana was about to leave the house when Freddie walked in. He was unshaven, his eyes wild-looking, his clothes crumpled – most out of character for a man as fastidious as Freddie Leon.

"My God!" Diana said, staring at her dishevelled husband. "You look as if you slept in your clothes. What hotel took you in looking like that?"

"Diana, leave me alone," Freddie said, pushing past her

on his way upstairs. As far as he was concerned, Diana was becoming more trouble than she was worth.

"Yes, Freddie, I will," she called after him. And set off to seal her future with Max Steele.

CHAPTER TWENTY-FOUR

ON THE beach in Malibu, two teenagers ran down to the sea. They were wearing black rubber wet-suits, their surfboards tucked under their arms.

"Great waves, dude," said one.

"Sweet," agreed the second one.

Just as they were about to enter the water, they noticed a fan of long blonde hair and one delicate arm tangled in seaweed.

They glanced at each other. "Holy shit! What's that?"

"Looks like a body."

Together they dragged the lifeless form out of the water and laid it on the sand.

It was a female. Gorgeous, blonde, and very, very naked.

Another murder.

Another beautiful day in L.A.

JACKIE COLLINS

The Santangelo Novels

Chances

£5.99

From the casinos of Las Vegas to the streets of New York, Chances was the name of the game . . . and everybody took them.

Gino Santangelo – a boy from the New York slums carves himself a crime empire that takes him all the way to the top.

His daughter, Lucky, proves herself to be as deadly as her father. Sensual and provocative, she is too much like him not to make a bid for his empire . . .

Chances spins through six decades like a giant roulette wheel, where the high stakes are on big money, dangerous sex and irresistible power.

JACKIE COLLINS

The Santangelo Novels

Lucky

£5.99

Like father, like daughter, winning runs in the family . . .

Daughter of one of the world's richest and most powerful men, wildly beautiful Lucky Santangelo is set on continuing the family tradition . . .

Sex and the rich fruits of crime are her aphrodisiacs. Power is the ultimate thrill – power over the Santangelo empire, power over the men of her choice.

Moving in the fast lane from Las Vegas to New York, Beverly Hills to a Greek island paradise, *Lucky* takes up where *Chances* left off. Winning is all that matters – and luck has nothing to do with it . . .

'If you take *Lucky* to the beach for sunbathing company, you may still be lying there reading when the moon comes up.'
Cosmopolitan

JACKIE COLLINS

The Santangelo Novels

Lady Boss

£5.99

Jackie Collins' sexiest creation is back – with a vengeance! Lucky Santangelo – she's ruthless, wild . . . and dangerous.

In *Chances* she showed how deadly a woman can be. In *Lucky* she showed what she had to do to win – 100 per cent of the time.

Now she's reaching for the ultimate prize – control over a major Hollywood studio. Control over the destinies of some of the richest and most powerful people on earth.

Lucky Santangelo is the Lady Boss. And what Lucky wants, Lucky always gets . . .